The Story of JESUS

Illustrated by Pascale Lafond

Many years ago, more than two thousand years ago, God sent His son, Jesus, down from Heaven to live among us here on earth. Jesus was born in a manger in Bethlehem. His mother, Mary, and her husband, Joseph, knew Jesus was very special.

Angels had told Mary and Joseph that Jesus was the Son of God. When Jesus was born, Shepherds and Wise Men came to see Him, because they also knew He was the Son of God. They were all filled with joy.

Even though there were many miracles related to the birth of Jesus and His early life, His presence went mostly unnoticed until He grew to be a man of about thirty years old.

At that time, there was a prophet named John the Baptist who told people that the Kingdom of Heaven was at hand. He encouraged them to turn from their sins and be baptized with water. Jesus went to be baptized by John. John recognized Him as the Christ he had been speaking of, and he told Jesus, "You should be baptizing me." But Jesus still wanted John to baptize Him, so John agreed.

When Jesus was being baptized, a dove descended from Heaven, and a voice from Heaven said, "This is My Son. I love Him, and I am very pleased with Him."

Now Jesus knew it was time to teach the people about God. Jesus would live among the people of Israel and teach them about God's love for them. Many people chose to follow Jesus as His disciples.

The first miracle Jesus performed was in front of His disciples at a wedding. Jesus' mother was also there. When the wine ran out, Jesus' mother told Him, "They have no wine."

Jesus had the servants bring Him six stone jugs filled with water, which He turned into wine. The wine He made was considered to be the best of the wedding party. In this way, Jesus performed His first miracle in honor of His mother. The miracle also helped His disciples believe in Him.

When Jesus was teaching, He told the people to love God and to love others as you love yourself. He said these two commandments are the most important to God, and everything else comes from following them.

While He lived among the people, Jesus performed many miracles. He healed sick people. He helped blind people see. He helped crippled people walk. Many people loved Jesus and followed Him wherever He went.

One time, thousands of people came to hear Jesus talk about God's love and how they should love each other. Nobody remembered to bring any food except for one little boy. The little boy gave Jesus his food, and through a miracle, Jesus fed thousands of people with just that one little boy's lunch.

While He did all these great things, Jesus reminded the people to care for each other, and to love each other, and to love God.

There were people in Israel who did not like Jesus. They wanted to have Him arrested. Jesus knew this was going to happen, so He had one last supper with His closest followers. He told them to not be afraid.

That night, after Jesus had shared supper with His disciples, He was praying in a garden when an army of soldiers came to arrest Him. His disciples wanted to defend Jesus, but He told them to not fight and agreed to go with the soldiers.

Jesus was brought before a Roman governor named Pontius Pilate to be sentenced. At that time, there was a holiday, and the custom was to set one prisoner free. Pontius Pilate offered to set Jesus free, but the crowd refused. When they refused, Pontius Pilate washed his hands in front of the crowd, claiming no responsibility for what was to happen to Jesus.

After Jesus' trial, He was made
to carry a cross up a hill. They put
Him up on that cross. They taunted and
ridiculed Him. Before he died on the cross,
Jesus asked God to forgive the people
who did this to Him.

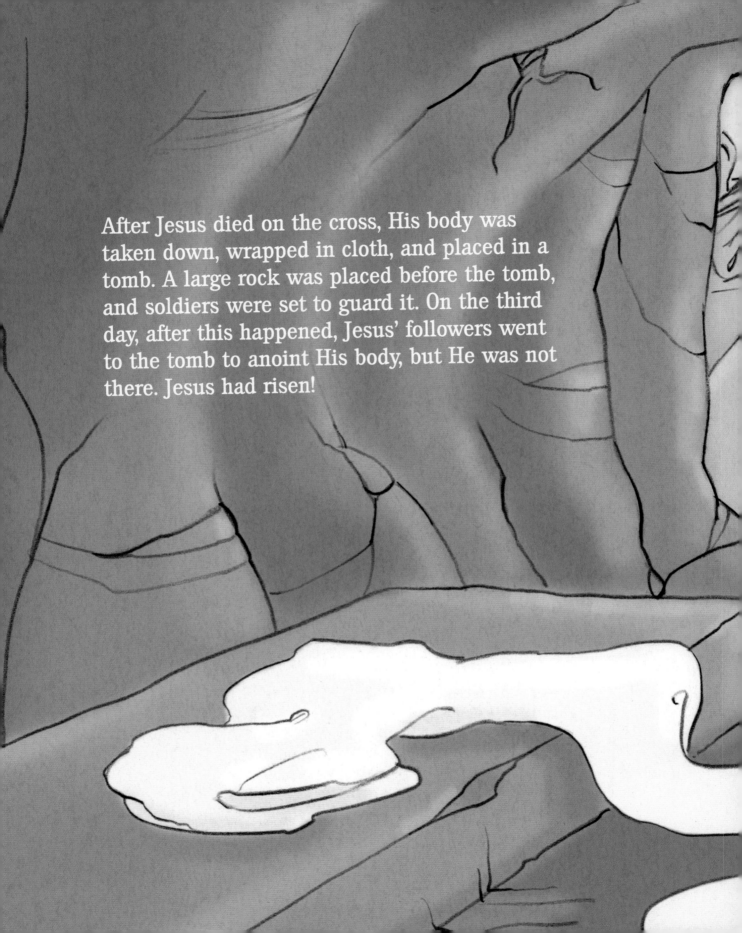

After Jesus died on the cross, His body was taken down, wrapped in cloth, and placed in a tomb. A large rock was placed before the tomb, and soldiers were set to guard it. On the third day, after this happened, Jesus' followers went to the tomb to anoint His body, but He was not there. Jesus had risen!

Jesus visited His friends and followers to let them know He had risen. Many people saw Him, and many of them went out to tell the world of the good news.

After appearing to His disciples, Jesus ascended into Heaven to be with His Father.

The story of Jesus coming down from Heaven, His life on earth, and His resurrection into Heaven has been shared for thousands of years by billions of people all over the world. It is the greatest story ever told.